Micah Loves Math!

Julia A. Royston

Illustrated by Cameron T. Wilson

BK

ROYSTON
Publishing

BK Royston Publishing LLC
P. O. Box 4321
Jeffersonville, IN 47131
http://www.bkroystonpublishing.com
bkroystonpublishing@gmail.com

502.802.5385

Cover Design and Illustrations: Cameron T. Wilson

ISBN-13:   978-1-959543-27-5

Printed in the USA

Dedication

I dedicate this book to any child that loves math. Be the math genius you were designed to be. Let's go!

Acknowledgements

I first acknowledge my divine and earthly team that is with me every step of the way. I couldn't do all of this without you.

I acknowledge all of the parents, godparents, foster parents, aunts, uncles, administrators, teachers, school counselors, social workers and case workers who are striving to support, help and guide children safely in this world. Thank you so much for your time, heart and service.

To everyone that shall read, share, purchase and recommend this book to any child, adult and/or organization. Thank you!

Micah Loves Math!

My name is Micah and I love math. Even at home during playtime, my parents observe me counting everything. I count my toys and their accessories even before I play with them.

I love numbers, counting or anything related to math. Even as a first grader, I can count to 500 and add two digit numbers.

My big brother Matthew often teases me and shows me the math that he is doing in school. He's in the sixth grade and I can't wait to be solving the problems that he is doing right now. I may not understand it but you just wait and see.

In the meantime, we count on the way to school. We count cars. Stop lights. People. He tells me what to count and I count as fast and I can while the bus is still moving. It is always fun to be with my brother. He is so smart but one day, I think I could be smarter than he is.

Even when my brother or my parents are not around, I am counting. In my room, my toys, clothes, books or anything else are a part of my counting and math journey.

I see the numbers on my mother's phone but I don't want to call anyone. I love to use her calculator app to see how many numbers I can get on the screen. I am still learning but one day, I'll get it right.

My dad's keys are just the beginning. I count everything that is in the garage. He tells me that I am his inventory specialist and know exactly how many things he has in the garage.

Numbers are my thing. What can I say?
I'm a math genius I think.

Not so fast. I've got a math test tomorrow.
Let's see what happens.

It didn't go well.

My brother Matthew asked, "What's wrong Micah?"

"I missed one problem today on the test because I didn't count correctly."

"Were you trying to finish first and missed something?"

"Yes, but I like to finish first."

"You finished first but wasn't careful to get the right answer. Was it worth it?" Matthew asked.

After our talk, I realized that I am smart in math for a 1st grader but there is still more math to learn.

I love Math and will continue to know and grow. What's your favorite subject in school? Mine will always be math. Why? Micah loves Math.

THE END

Thank you for reading the book, "Micah Loves Math." I hope you enjoyed it.

Think for a minute. What's your favorite subject in school?

No matter the subject always take your time. Do your best and you will truly succeed. Let's go!

To connect with Julia A. Royston, visit www.juliaakroyston.com or email her at bkroystonpublishing@gmail.com.

More Books by Julia A. Royston

Julia Royston Books
www.juliaroystonstore.com

How Many Objects Are on This Page?

_____

How Many Objects Are on This Page?

_____

How Many Objects Are on This Page?

_____

How Many Objects Are on This Page?

_____

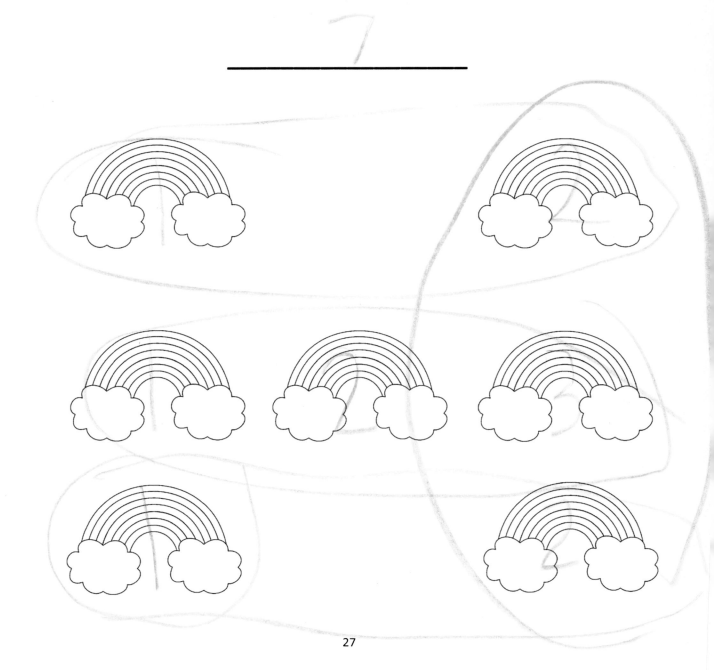

How Many Objects Are on This Page?

_____

Made in the USA
Monee, IL
05 March 2023

29145203R00021